To every Grumbly who has ever
admitted they were wrong ~ J K

To Angel ~ C S

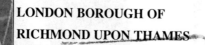
LITTLE TIGER PRESS LTD,

an imprint of the Little Tiger Group

1 Coda Studios,

189 Munster Road,

London SW6 6AW

www.littletiger.co.uk

First published in Great Britain 2020

Text copyright © John Kelly 2020

Illustrations copyright © Carmen Saldaña 2020

John Kelly and Carmen Saldaña have asserted their rights

to be identified as the author and illustrator of this work

under the Copyright, Designs and Patents Act, 1988

A CIP catalogue record for this book is available

from the British Library

Printed in China · LTP/1400/2940/0120

2 4 6 8 10 9 7 5 3 1

MEET THE
GRUMBLIES

JOHN KELLY

CARMEN SALDAÑA

LiTTLE TiGER
LONDON

In the land of Grumbly, life was easy-peasy.
The bread bushes were full of rolls, squidgy-fruit hung
from every tree, and the pond was full of fizzy juice.
    So the Grumblies had lots of spare time to sit around and . . .

... ARGUE!
"OGG!" said Grumble-Stick. "STICK BEST!"
"AGG!" said Grumble-Rope. "ROPE BEST!"
"IGG!" grunted Grumble-Mud. "MUD BEST!"

They were still arguing when
CRAASSHHHH!
a HUGE, hungry creature STOMPED
out of the forest.

"GOBBLESTOMP!"
cried the Grumblies.
The hairy beast was STOMPING
towards their bread bushes!

"OGG! STOP!" cried Grumble-Stick, and the brave little Grumbly threw some sticks at the Gobblestomp. But they just bounced off the Gobblestomp's thick coat as it CHOMPED all the bread rolls.

Then it spotted the squidgy-fruit trees.

"AGG! STOP!" cried Grumble-Rope, bravely lassoing the Gobblestomp's leg. But the Gobblestomp ignored the rope, munched most of the squidgy-fruit . . .

then STOMPED off towards the juice pond.

"IGG! STOP!" cried Grumble-Mud.

In a flash, the brave Grumbly had dug a moat in the mud.

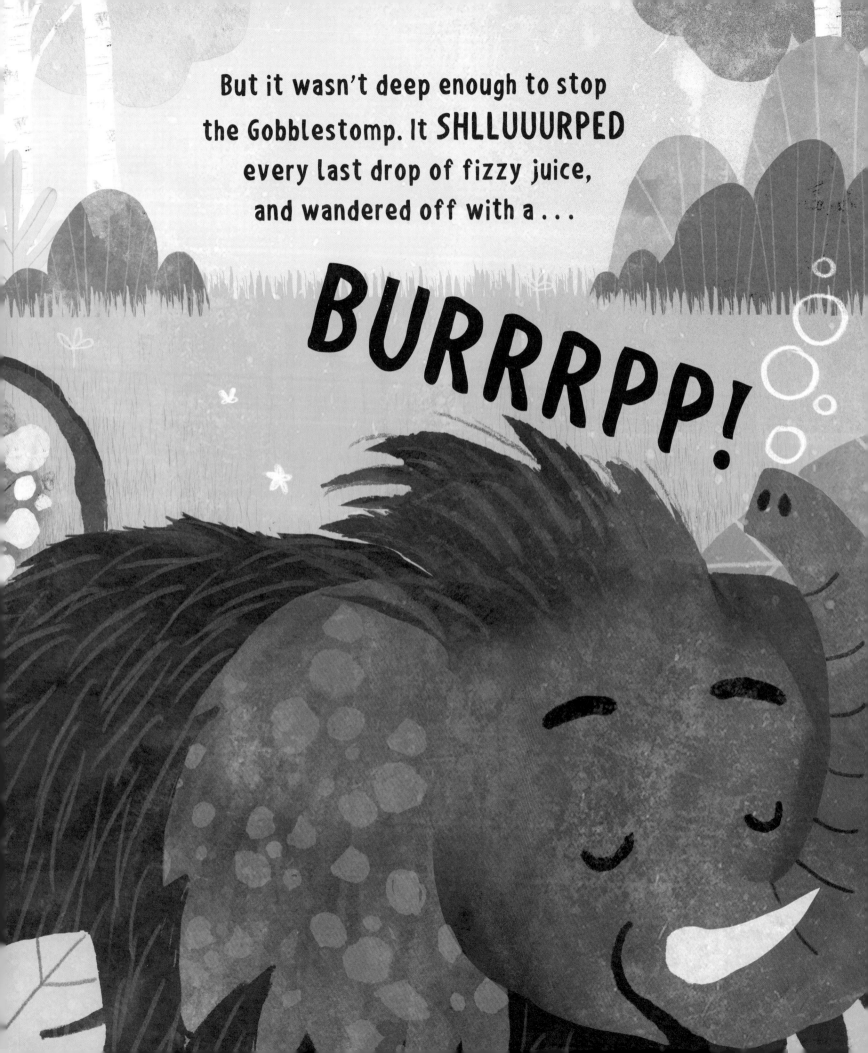

But it wasn't deep enough to stop the Gobblestomp. It **SHLLUUURPED** every last drop of fizzy juice, and wandered off with a . . .

BURRRPP!

"OGG!" sighed Grumble-Stick.
"STICK NOT BEST!"

"AGG!" agreed Grumble-Rope.
"ROPE NOT BEST!"

"IGG!" grunted Grumble-Mud.
"MUD NOT BEST!"

For the first time EVER, the Grumblies stopped arguing and made a plan.

They worked through the night, and in the morning marched off to face the Gobblestomp . . . together.

The Gobblestomp was fast asleep and snoring loudly.
"OGG! AGG! IGG!" shouted the Grumblies.

The Gobblestomp opened one sleepy eye.

Then it jumped up and chased them through the forest . . .

STOMP! CRASH! STOMP!

and into the village . . .

STOMP! CRASH! STOMP!

when it suddenly stopped and sniffed!

The Gobblestomp had spotted the
last few squidgy-fruits.
"GOBBLE-MUNCH!" it trumpeted,
and stomped over to the pile.
But before it could MUNCH one there was a . . .

CRACK . . .

SNAP . . .

...CRASH!

The Gobblestomp fell through a stick trapdoor and into a HUGE rope net at the bottom of a deep, muddy pit.

"OGG! AGG! IGG!" sang the Grumblies
together. "Grumblies best!"

But then a sad

"GOBBLEY-SNIFF!"

came from the hole.

The Grumblies peered over the edge.
The Gobblestomp didn't look dangerous any more.
It just looked sad. And maybe a little hungry!
   "POOR GOBBLESTOMP!" said the Grumblies.

Then, "OGG! AGG! IGG!" they sang as they helped the Gobblestomp out of the hole and invited it for dinner.

In return, the Gobblestomp promised to never STOMP or CHOMP or SHLURP in the Grumblies' village again.

In fact, the Gobblestomp
even started helping out!

GRUMBLY
VILLAGE
PUBLIC
POOL

Which is handy, because now that the Grumblies have stopped arguing so much, they've got some pretty **BIG** plans!